THE CLONING OF PLEASURE

An Erotic Adventure

By

J. Ollie Manoeuvre

Audrey came sweeping into his room after school with a heavy step shedding his outer layers with a swiftness that could only spell one thing. He was in a right state from the constant pressure and bullying he put up with at that wretched school of his and there was only one thing that was going to cool him down.

Audrey had been exploring his body now for the past year and he had become very good at it. Through careful experimentation he had discovered the various buttons and levers which would produce certain definable effects and he knew how to manipulate these buttons like a conductor playing a symphony. On this occasion he knew just where he would begin—first he checked the hallway to make sure no-one else was home, then he carefully closed and locked his bedroom door stripping naked with a languorous, melancholy speed. He paused to admire himself in the mirror—he was very white, almost translucent like his skin was made of fine paper, his auburn hair hung in long semi-curled tresses that rested delicately on

3

his thin shoulders. His body was almost hairless barring a small smattering under the armpits and a soft downy bush of curly hair that grew around him ample cock. His eyes lingered over this last appendage as he took in its meaty girth and respectable length. Half-hard he was able to really take in what he had to offer, and it was glorious. Next, he set the mood by lighting a series of black-wax candles that gave off a faint orange glow that caused his white skin to flicker in and out of focus like an old film, then he put on some music, a soft jazz affair that made him feel sophisticated and debonaire. He didn't know much about jazz, but he had found a few records at a garage sale and these always served him well when he got himself all heated up like this—the modern rock and roll records all the other kids were listening to just did nothing for him. Of course, when things got really exciting or he was planning on taking his time with himself, there was always the option of a Beethoven symphony, but this particular evening he had decided to stick with the tried-and-true jazz records that had earned a firm place in his erotic repertoire.

He moved over to the bed and opened the top drawer of his dresser. It was here that he kept his 'tools of the trade' and he had some ideas about what was to come next. First, he selected a ball-gag and strapped it around his head savouring the soft silicone taste of the rubber ball in his mouth. His jaw clicked slightly as he forced it in and he felt the vibration of the gag as he moaned slightly enjoying the feeling of self-imposed helplessness. Next, he found a pair of silver clips which he positioned on his small red nipples and tightened until they were almost excruciating. He moaned again and smiled internally at the muffled sound that came from his stuffed mouth. He was fully erect now with his long hard cock coming up to his belly button and twitching slightly with each tensing of the muscles. The cool air played around the head as a pearl of lubricant squeezed out and coated the pink bulb. He could feel his testicle coil up tighter in expectation.

Lastly from the drawer he selected a realistic looking dildo about the size of his own penis and with a slight curve in the shaft so that it was shaped somewhat like a banana. He pressed the false cock lovingly against his cheek and weighed the thing in his hands testing the girth with his fingers and caressing the veiny shaft. He fumbled around in the drawer and came out with a jar of Vaseline with he rubbed onto the dildo with breathless haste, taking another scoop of Vaseline and rubbing into his twitching asshole with a slow circular pull. He prepared himself for the eventual entry of the dildo by inserting one finger up to the second knuckle and twisting it around in a circle feeling for his prostate with a hooked 'come-hither' motion. Once he found it, he inserted a second finger feeling his sphincter stretch as the newcomer came in up to the second knuckle. He moaned again and tensed his pectorals so that the nipple clamps renewed their assault. The time was right— he pulled out his fingers slowly and began to work the dildo into his ass with a soft

corkscrew motion grinding the fake dick
into his ass with a firm and solid pressure.
He worked it in slowly all the way up to
the flanged end and bit down on the ball-
gag. He felt himself tightening up to a ball
of white light—a white heat passed through
his body and he shivered as an orgasmic
spasm passed through him sending arcs of
jism out onto the bed. Three spurts and
Audrey collapsed down into a small pool of
his own cum, his asshole jerking and
forcing the dildo back out onto the bed.
Audrey lay there for five whole minutes
breathing heavily into his rubber gag.
Slowly he came to his senses and
unscrewed the nipple clamps and undid the
ball-gag. His tender nipples responded with
delightful pain to their new freedom and
the cold air—his jaw fell into place and left
an empty feeling in his mouth that was
echoed by his asshole. He carefully cleaned
his tools and put them back in the top
drawer of his dresser, closing it with a
tender hand before laying back on his bed
to savour the post orgasmic feeling of

contentedness that had swept through his body.

He must have drifted off because the next half-hour in missing completely from his memory banks. He woke with a start to hear the rumble of a vehicle parking outside. At first, he thought nothing of it, assuming that it was simply one other of his parents home from their long day at the office, but soon, as he lay in his slumbering state, he began to grow wary as the engine did not cut off instead idling outside his very window. He got up and dressed quickly in a thin t-shirt and an old pair of blue jeans before walking cautiously over to the window and pulling back the curtain. There, parked under the streetlight outside, and idling away was an unmarked white van with dark tinted windows. "Must be the telephone company or something to do with the electrics" he mused to himself, but still something seemed out of place and he kept his eye on the vehicle for some time. When, after a period of ten minutes, nothing happened with the strange car, he decided that he was being silly and left his room to venture into the kitchen and find something to eat.

In the kitchen his suspicion was again aroused as he saw that the back door to the semi-detached had been unbolted and was left slightly ajar. He called out to see if his parents were home. No answer. He called out the obligatory "is anybody there?" and was met, as expected, with no answer. He tried to push all thoughts of anything untoward out of his mind and focus on getting the snack he had come downstairs for, but his nerves were on edge. Something was definitely wrong. Just then it clicked—a black bag came swooping down from behind and the strong smell of ether flooded his brain. Complete and total blackout.

Audrey came to in the back of the unmarked white van, at least that is where he assumed he was from the engine hum and the slow rhythmic pulsing like a car on a highway. He had no way of telling how long he had been here driving or how far he had come. The black bag had been removed from his head, but the windows had been completely blacked out and all there was to see were two stocky men in rough army-surplus combat gear and domino masks which did little to hide their identities, but as they were unknown to Audrey, this did not matter in the slightest.

Audrey tried moving but found that his legs and arms were tied with a hemp rope. He struggled slightly but the knots held fast. At first he felt panic welling up inside of himself putting pressure on the inside wall of his chest, but pretty soon the remnants of the ether came swooping back to placate him. He even began to find the pressure of the hemp ropes somewhat pleasurable. It reminded him of his moods at home in his room where he had experimented with tying himself up. He had never been this successful at it, always needing at least one free hand to tie and untie the knots, but he was now finding that the sensation was not entirely unpleasant. He felt himself beginning to grow hard and he felt his face burn a deep red with embarrassment. He knew that his

blue jeans would be sticking out at the fly
about now and in his prone position this
would be on display for the two men to see.
It was not long before one of the two men
did in fact notice. He nudged his
compatriot and pointed down with a smirk
that lifted his domino mask higher up onto
his spacious forehead. "Looks like he likes
it…"

"I'll say."

"We better help him out."

"I think it's best."

One of the men reached over and
rolled Audrey onto his side so that he was
facing the two men directly. He was fully
erect now and the fabric at the front of his
jeans was straining under the pressure of
his sizeable cock. The man who had rolled
him over fumbled with the button of
Audrey's jeans and the fly and soon
succeeded in opening the front of his pants
so that Audrey's cock sprang forth like a
jack in the box.

"Well, look at what we got here!"

"He's a big one, that's for sure."

The second man reached over and touched Audrey's cock with a rough, calloused hand. Audrey winced backwards but felt a jolt of electric excitement run through him that was not unpleasurable. The man began to masturbate Audrey with a slow, gentle pull putting a firm pressure on Audrey's shaft and sliding the smooth skin up and down the length of his penis. After a few strokes of this Audrey groaned and the man grinned a bucktooth smile.

"I think he likes it!"

He stopped suddenly withdrawing his hand and spitting liberally into his palm. He manoeuvred his hand back down now slick with spit and began to masturbate Audrey with a more vigorous motion. The car began to rock and sway as if it had suddenly moved off road and was careening down a dirt track—the bumps and jolts of the uneven road leapt through the man's arms and hand and into Audrey's cock. Audrey began to salivate slightly and moan low under his breath. Suddenly the car pulled to an abrupt halt and the man squeezed tight pushing his wet hand all the way down to the base of his penis pushing up against his pelvic bone and tickling against his soft mound of brown pubic hair. Audrey shot out a spurt of hot cum which flew through the air and hit the man on his camo-print jacket. The man withdrew his hand and wiped the glob of fresh semen from his coat and slowly lifted his fingers to his lips sucking Audrey's seed from them and smacking his lips.

"Yes, he's going to be a good one, that's for sure."

*

Audrey was untied and taken from the car into a large stone building in the middle of what appeared to be a forest clearing. There were no streetlights, no paved road, and no other buildings in sight. Once inside, Audrey found himself in a large room with a folding table like one sees in a doctor's office, a filing cabinet, a series of shelves containing a number of instruments and jars of unknown purpose, and a long mirror taking up one wall which Audrey could not help but think was one of those two-way mirrors you find in police station interrogation rooms. He was left alone in this room for about half an hour before someone finally came. A small man in a white coat with steel-rimmed glasses carrying a clipboard appeared from beyond a door situated in a far corner of the room.

"Mr uh Carson, so nice of you to join us."

The man glanced down at his clipboard to be sure of the name.

Audrey was dumbfounded. So this was clearly pre-arranged, but by whom and to what purpose? He didn't have time to think over these questions very long because soon two more small men in white coats looking very much like the first, so close they could be brothers, appeared and began undressing Audrey. They did not speak but simply moved him like he was a mannequin or shop dummy pulling at his clothes and leaving his naked standing there in the cold air of the room seeing his reflection in the long mirrr on the far wall. Soon he was left alone again standing naked in the centre of the room. His clothes had been taken away by the team of small men so he could not redress himself and he had nothing to occupy himself apart from walking the length of the room and inspecting the instruments and jars he found on the shelves. The instruments were all made of the same material—a sort of steel-like metal that glowed with a faint green hum and seemed warm to the touch despite the cold air of the room. Audrey could not tell what any of the instruments might be for, but they looked medical in nature and judging by the clinical nature his surroundings he was sure that he had wandered into some sort of bad b-movie sci-fi script. "Any second now and they'll start probing me," thought Audrey attempting to lighten his mood with a bout of gallows humour, but the sentiment seemed to real and close to home to bring any laughter.

Soon enough, another man in a white coat did enter the door and check his clipboard before saying "Mr uh Carson, if you would follow me to the table please, my sponsors are eager to begin the uh procedure."

With nothing else to do, Audrey did as the man said and went over to the folding table that stood in the centre of the room. On closer inspection Audrey noticed that this table had been modified somewhat. It was host to a myriad of straps and stirrups in all manner of positions— Audrey shuddered to think what these might be used for, but he was certain that he would soon find out.

"Please lay down on the table."

Once again, Audrey did as he was told.

"Now, when you uh *touch yourself* what are the uh *images* used?"

"I'm sorry?"

"Hurrumph, the *images* lad—do you picture boys, girls, something else entirely?"

"Oh, well, boys usually—sometimes I think about my classmates and—"

"That's quite alright, thank you very much. We'll take care of that right away."

The man produced a device from some hidden recess of the room and began attaching electrodes to Audrey's temples and around his forehead. Audrey did not resist—he figured, what choice did he have?

Soon enough, the man finished placing the electrodes and switched on the device to which they were attached. He began to fiddle with a series of knobs and dials and the machine clicked and whirred like a small bird. Within moments images began to flood into Audrey's mindscreen. Taut muscular boys in the prime of their youth oiling each other up in Greco-Roman pantomime, pulling at each other's togas and goosing each other with nimble playful fingers. Audrey felt a slow electric stirring in his loins and the images became more intense and focussed. He could vaguely sense the man reading a list of figures from a screen attached to the electrode device and fine-tuning his knobs and dials. He was more aware, however, of how the images in his mind were shifting and pulsing becoming people he knew in his favourite sexual positions. He could feel their hot breath playing about his neck and tragus, he could almost feel the touch of their hands as they came close and offered their bodies to him. Audrey felt himself growing intolerably hard—he began to reach out a hand to take care of himself but found that he could not move. With an effort he managed to wrench his attention away from the images in his mind and found that during his distraction he had been strapped down to the table by his ankles and wrists. His arms were firmly locked by his sides so that he could not move them at all and his feet were suspended a little wider than shoulder width above the bed so that his ass was fully exposed to the air. He noticed too that there were more people in the room with him now. A team of what appeared to be scientists had flooded in and were talking amongst themselves and fiddling with various instruments picked up from the shelves. Audrey fell back into reverie and felt the soft skin of his classmates rubbing up against his thighs, the electric hairs stood up on his legs and he buzzed with excitement. He envisioned Eric, a boy he rather fancied, naked and greased like a Roman gladiator walking up to him in his prone position and sliding his hard cock up his tight asshole with a soft corkscrew motion—Audrey wrenched himself away again and found that his dreams were closer to reality than he expected. One of the scientists had brought one of the metallic devices close to his rectum and had begun penetrating him with a soft but forceful pressure. The sensation was not unpleasant, in fact Audrey was quite enjoying it, and he let out a low moan that did not seem to phase the team of scientists in the slightest. The man with the device began to work it in to Audrey's ass and twisting it round and round. Audrey felt his prostate stimulated with the warm pressure of the metal instrument and he felt his nuts coiling up and tightening in anticipation of immanent orgasm. Suddenly he felt a sharp cutting pain deep in his colon—once again this was not unpleasurable and Audrey found himself quite enjoying it after the initial shock had worn off.

A muttered word was passed back and forth between the scientists and the device was removed roughly. Audrey saw that a small cutting of his colon had been taken by the device and was suspended at the front of the metallic tube by three sharp silver prongs. Audrey felt himself cumming involuntarily, shooting arcs of jism out into the cold clinical air of the large room. His cum shot through the air and landed on the small cube of flesh that had just been cut out of him which seemed to please the scientist holding the instrument immensely. He made a motion to one of the other whitecoats and the second man rushed off to gather a jar from one of the shelves. The small parcel of flesh was deposited in this jar and covered with a thin blue liquid that seemed to smoke and fog up on contact with the cutting.

The electrodes were removed from Audrey's head and he felt himself returning more fully to the present. It no longer required any effort to stay focussed on the here and now and the images of his classmates were rapidly fading into old memories. His arms and legs were unstrapped and the team of scientists began to disappear one by one through the door at the far end of the room. One of them placed the jar filled with Audrey's sperm and colon cutting on a shelf before leaving. The flesh seemed to be pulsing with a strange life of its own. It appeared to have doubled in size since it was first taken and was growing at an ever increasing rate. Audrey watched it in a half daze from his position on the foldable bed and was caught by surprise when the door opened again and yet another scientist came bustling in the take the sample and transfer it to a large vat on wheels that had been brought in for the purpose. Once the cutting had been placed in the vat and the scientist had disappeared again, the cutting began to grow at an even more rapid pace taking on the definite form of a living creature. Limbs were beginning to form as well as the rudimentary shape of a spine and ribcage. The longer Audrey stared, the more complete the creature became and the more eerily familiar it was to him. There was something about this strange animal growing from a cutting of his own flesh that reverberated deep within his own memories, but he could not place where he had seen such a creature before.

After about an hour of growth it suddenly became clear to Audrey. The reason the creature had seemed so unnervingly familiar was that it was growing into a mirror image of himself. Right down to the birthmark on his right hip (left hip on the creature floating suspended in its vat of liquid), everything was present and accounted for. Audrey was laying there staring at himself in a different skin—a second Audrey dumb as fish just floating there in a vat of liquid. After the initial shock of this wore off, Audrey slid off the table and moved over to inspect the strange creature. As he got closer, he noticed that the liquid in the vat was slowly draining—within twenty minutes there would be nothing left. So, Audrey watched and waited wondering what would happen when the liquid finally ran out.

When the liquid passed away from Audrey-Two's face the clone creature breathed in a deep breath of fresh air and began to flail its limbs wildly. This panicked Audrey and he decided that he would have to free the creature before it hurt itself. He searched to vat for some sort of release valve or controls and soon found a panel of buttons. He pushed at the first button he found and sure enough, the liquid drained away at a more rapid pace and the front of the vat swung open on an invisible hinge. The Audrey clone fell out and down onto the floor in a crumpled heap. Audrey bent down over himself and lifted him up carrying him to the bed where he could get a closer look. The clone was slowly coming

to its senses and seemed to recognise
Audrey with a primal recognition. He
reached out a slender white hand and
touched Audrey's face with a tender
motion.

Gazing at his naked mirror image
and feeling his own soft touch brought back
memories of his bedroom and the sweet
tender embrace of his own body. Here was
a chance to press the buttons and play the
symphony in another flesh. He felt himself
grow hard again and looking down saw that
his clone had done the same. He reached
out and took one of his clone's nipples
between his thumb and forefinger and
twisted roughly. He saw the clone wince in
pleasurable pain. He saw his cock jump and
stand further to attention. He pushed his
clone off the bed and into a standing
position and knelt before him admiring his
own cock from a position he had never
before been able to obtain. He saw the
slight curve of the shaft, the meaty girth,
and the slow twitching pulse of blood close
to his own face and watched with wonder
as a pearl of lubricant squeezed out from

the top of the head and coated the pink bulb. He took his own penis in his mouth and began to suck, slowly at first savouring the taste of his own salty pre-ejaculate, then faster and faster until he could hear his own breath quicken and feel with nuts tighten to a spring and explode inside his mouth. He tasted his salty cum with relish sucking hard on the head of his penis to draw out every last drop. Then, satisfied with the pleasure he had just given himself, he stood up and turned his clone around bending him over so that his arms were resting supported by the folding table and his hips were at a right angle with the floor. Audrey spat on his cock and on his hand and used his hand to work the spit into his clone's asshole. He slowly spread his own ass cheeks and looked with wonder at the rosebud of his asshole gaping open like a mouth just waiting to devour his member.

He pushed his penis, slick with his own spit, into his clone's ass and began to pump wildly losing himself in the movement and the moment of passion. Suddenly the lights went out and the two

Audrey's found themselves encased in darkness. The mirror along the far wall lit up like a cinema screen and Audrey saw himself there fucking his own double roughly from behind. This image replicated from every angle and played out over the screen as if it had a life of its own. Not simply a reflection but a living breathing piece of work that fucked itself up the ass from every conceivable angle. Soon these images of Audrey were pulsing away out of time to Audrey's own pumps and were moaning their own moans and grinning their own grins of pleasure. One by one they pulsed outwards and pushed through the screen into the room with Audrey with a wet sucking sound like a finger through a mould of jelly. The room filled with Audrey's in all manner of reflection—birthmarks on the right and left, sharp hips jutting this way and that until it became impossible to tell the original from the replicas. And they all joined in fucking one another, sucking each other's cocks and tasting the salty cum as it spurted about the room. Audreys were collapsing spent in heaps folded over the bodies of their counterparts, Audreys were grabbing at the cocks of other Audreys and jerking until their faces were splattered with warm semen. There was a veritable orgy of Audreys and the fucking continued from every angle in every position under the sun. This went on for hours and hours until the very last Audrey collapsed spent and wasted in a crumpled heap on the ground.

The Audreys fell asleep in this way in a big pile of twisted sweaty flesh. The memory files are blank from this point forwards.

THE END